Designed by John Sazaklis

TM & © 2018 Nintendo. All rights reserved.
Published in the United States by Random House Children's Books,
a division of Penguin Random House LLC, 1745 Broadway, New York, NY 10019,
and in Canada by Penguin Random House Canada Limited, Toronto.
Random House and the colophon are registered trademarks of
Penguin Random House LLC.

rhcbooks.com

ISBN 978-1-5247-7265-9

MANUFACTURED IN CHINA

10 9 8 7 6 5 4 3 2 1

THE LEGEND OF
ZELDA™

LINK'S BOOK OF
ADVENTURE

BY
STEVE FOXE

Random House 🏠 New York

A HERO'S JOURNEY

Throughout many eras, the fearless hero LINK has summoned his courage to fight the menace known as GANON and defend the KINGDOM OF HYRULE.

The humble HYLIAN uses his wits and his sword to overcome obstacles in his way and discover the truth path to becoming a hero.

Link wields the mighty **MASTER SW0RD** in his quest to oppose Ganon's evil forces. What weapon would you take with you on your epic journey? What are its special powers? Draw yourself and your heroic weapon.

spike claw spear

spike, drain

saw

Spike zora sword

During most of his quests, Link must collect special items to aid him in overcoming challenges. With the mysterious SHEIKAH SLATE, Link can unlock ancient runes to serve the same purposes as some of those items.

ANCIENT RUNES

- **MAGNESIS** allows Link to move heavy metal objects, which is often crucial in solving difficult puzzle dungeons.

- **REMOTE BOMB** allows Link to place both square and round bombs that can damage enemies, blow up structures, and clear rubble.

- **STASIS** is one of the most complicated runes. It allows Link to stop the flow of time. If he strikes an object in this state, it will store up energy that sends it flying when released.

- **CRYONIS** raises pillars of frozen water to create new stepping-stones for Link—or to open up new paths.

- **CAMERA** helps Link document his journey and add facts about enemies, items, and locations to his Hyrule Compendium.

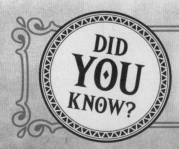

DID YOU KNOW?

The Sheikah Slate is Link's key item in 2017's *The Legend of Zelda: Breath of the Wild.* Its design resembles a Hyrulean version of the Nintendo Switch console or the Wii U GamePad!

Link becomes quite the chef during his adventures in *Breath of the Wild*. He fishes, forages for fresh ingredients, and cooks tasty food over a campfire to restore his health and stamina after battle or to temporarily boost his abilities. Below are a few of Link's favorite meals.

VEGETABLE OMELET

MADE WITH:
▷ Any vegetable, herb, or flower
▷ Bird eggs
▷ Goat butter
▷ Rock salt

HEARTY SALMON RISOTTO

MADE WITH:
▷ Salmon
▷ Rock salt
▷ Hylian rice
▷ Goat butter

APPLE PIE

MADE WITH:
▷ Apples
▷ Goat butter
▷ Cane sugar
▷ Tabantha wheat

MONSTER CURRY

MADE WITH:
▷ Monster extract
▷ Goron spice
▷ Hylian rice

Follow these simple instructions to make an adventurer's trail mix. (Then go eat—you're probably starving after all this talk of food!)

ADVENTURER'S JOURNEY TRAIL MIX

▷ Sunflower seeds
▷ Pumpkin seeds
▷ Dark chocolate chips
▷ Pretzel sticks
▷ Raisins or dried cranberries
▷ Almonds (optional)

Mix equal amounts of each ingredient in a large bowl. Take this healthy, hearty snack with you on your expeditions!

What kinds of food would you take with you on your hero's journey? List them below.

PRINCESS ZELDA gathered four powerful Champions to defeat the scourge of CALAMITY GANON. Find their names, as well as the words at the top of the next page, in the puzzle. Look forward, backward, up, down, and diagonally!

DARUK

URBOSA

REVALI

ZELDA

MIPHA

COURAGE ▲ GANON ▲ GERUDO ▲ GORON ▲ HYLIAN ▲ HYRULE
KOROK ▲ LINK ▲ POWER ▲ RITO ▲ SHEIKAH ▲ WISDOM ▲ ZORA

```
R E W O P R A T Z B L O V U K
K N A I L Y H L O C T S Y O Z
E U H X H W P W R N Q M R N U
D Z R G M T I I A W Y O S U V
R E V A L I M L M Y K D D M S
W M Q Z D K A C W Q U S Z P H
M G Q L S D K W O A L I N K E
I E W G L Y Q E N U G W N J I
G W L E A F P A I E R S M N K
O L Z U Z N S C R O A A N F A
R L Y H R O O U G F C S G V H
O R M T B Y D N P V S N X E A
N Y I R N O H J T P J Q T R E
I M U T D B W M P L X G B E O
X F H Q O S V R D I E K X N F
```

See pages 64 and 65 for all answers.

11

The world in
The Legend of Zelda: Skyward Sword
is lush and colorful, full of bright skies,
teeming forests, and sandblasted deserts.
Take inspiration from nature to
complete this scene.

Link and Zelda are
companions and classmates in SKYLOFT.
Find a friend of your own and play this game.
Take turns connecting two dots with a straight line.
If the line you draw completes a box,
put your initials in it and
take another turn.

Count one point for squares containing
your initials. Whoever has more points
at the end of the game wins.

Link's adventure among the clouds features new and familiar faces alike. Can you name some of the people and creatures Link encounters as he journeys through the wide-open skies? Use the clues to complete this crossword.

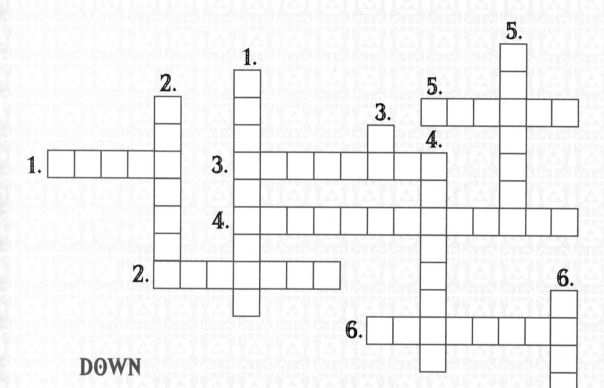

DOWN

1. A spiderlike enemy with a grisly abdomen.
2. Skeletal foes who wield two swords.
3. The spirit within the Goddess Sword.
4. Link's foe down below.
5. The color of Link's steed.
6. Link's royal classmate and childhood friend.

ACROSS

1. The name of the goddess Zelda plays in the Wing Ceremony.
2. A series of islands floating high above the surface.
3. Link bonds with this kind of bird.
4. The black beast that haunts Link's dreams.
5. The demon lord behind it all.
6. The sacred relic made of three triangles.

The vain LORD GHIRAHIM rules the land below Skyloft.
He seeks to capture Zelda and use her divine spirit to resurrect his
master, DEMISE. Although he initially dismisses Link as nothing more
than a pest, he soon discovers that Link has the soul of a true hero.

Help Link face his foe by using this grid to draw Lord Ghirahim.

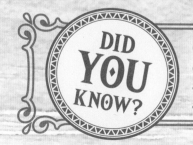

Ghirahim appears as a boss fight and playable character in the game *Hyrule Warriors,* and as a trophy in *Super Smash Bros. for Nintendo 3DS* and *Super Smash Bros. for Wii U.*

IMPA is a member of the **SHEIKAH** tribe,
the dedicated guardians of the goddess **HYLIA** and her mortal incarnations.
So loyal is Impa that she travels through a Gate of Time into the far past to protect
Hylia's mortal form. Impa's forehead is marked by an important tattoo.
Use the alphabet code below to reveal what Impa's tattoo represents.

A	B	C	D	E	F	G	H	I	J	K	L	M	N	O	P	Q	R	S	T	U	V	W	X	Y	Z
Z	Y	X	W	V	U	T	S	R	Q	P	O	N	M	L	K	J	I	H	G	F	E	D	C	B	A

H S V R P Z S
S h e i k a h

V B V
e y e

H B N Y L O
S y m B O L

18

Draw and describe a symbol that is meaningful to you.

LOFTWING LOOPS

Everyone in the floating island city of Skyloft bonds
with their own **LOFTWING**—it is said that Skyloftians don't consider
themselves complete until they've met their partner bird.

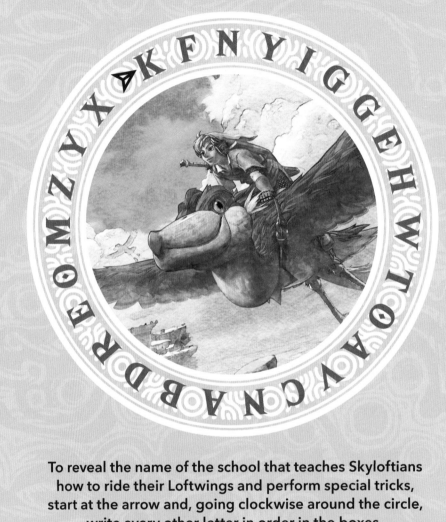

To reveal the name of the school that teaches Skyloftians
how to ride their Loftwings and perform special tricks,
start at the arrow and, going clockwise around the circle,
write every other letter in order in the boxes.

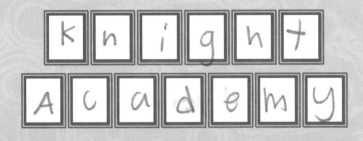

k n i g h t

A c a d e m y

What kind of animal would you
choose to bond with, and why?
Would you slither around on top of a giant
snake or swim the seas with a mighty whale?
Describe your perfect companion animal.

DID YOU KNOW?

The Legend of Zelda: Skyward Sword is the first
and only installment released exclusively on the
Nintendo Wii console. Its unique combat allowed
players to swing their Wii Remotes like swords!

Throughout Link's quest, terrifying shadow beasts travel through portals to menace him. To protect Hyrule from these dark denizens of the TWILIGHT REALM, Link takes the form of a wolf and enlists the help of MIDNA, a mysterious member of the magic-wielding TWILI race.

Study the scene on the left for up to three minutes; then cover the page and try to answer these questions.

1. How many shadow beasts are swarming Link?

2. What color are the patterns covering the shadow beasts?

3. Midna has similar symbols covering her body. What color is her pattern?

4. Wolf Link has a broken chain locked around one of his legs. Which leg is it?

5. There are three characters in the background of the image. Is Princess Zelda on the right side or the left side?

6. Human Link is holding a weapon in the background. What weapon is he holding, and in which hand is he holding it?

7. Midna's crown blocks one of her eyes. Which eye is still visible?

KNOW YOUR ENEMY

During the struggle with the Twilight Realm, Link faces terrifying versions of his longtime enemies, as well as unknown horrors. Find your way through this grid using the names of Link's fearsome foes. Each word follows the next with no space between them. Move up, down, left, or right, but not diagonally.

BOKOBLIN - DYNALFOS - KEESE - STALHOUND - GOHMA - KARGAROK - DEKU BABA
TORCH SLUG - SHADOW BEAST - SKULLTULA - STALFOS - SKULLWALLTULA - ARMOS
REDEAD KNIGHT - MOLDORM - LIZALFOS - FREEZARD - GUAY - GHOUL RATS - DODONGO
BUBBLE - SKULL KID - AERALFOS - DEKU TOAD - DARKHAMMER - DARKNUT

```
B O K F O S G O H M A D E A D
X K O L A N Y G R A K E I N K
R E B L I N D A R O K R G H T
E L A L U T L L A W L L U K S
M I Z A L F O S K E E S E S T
M B A B U K E D D N U O H L A
A A L T U L A S T A L F O S
H S U R E T B B U B D R A Z T
K H K A A S L E D O D O N E O
R A S L D A M R A Y A U G E R
A D T F A E O S S K U G O R C
D O S O O V Q I Z X L L G F H
M W A S T U K E D T U K U L S
R B E M T S D A R K N I U Q A
O D L O A R L U O H G D T L L
```

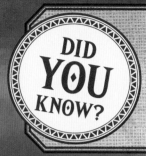

Dangerous monsters block Link's passage through the temples and dungeons of Hyrule. He must rely on all his skills and weapons to overcome their unique challenges and continue with his quest.

Decipher the names of these beasts.
Each Rupee stands for a missing vowel.

A E I O U

1. This high-flying creature menaces the birdlike Oocca race in the City in the Sky.

◊RG◊R◊K

ARGOROK

2. This boss guards the Temple of Time and attacks with a powerful laser.

◊RM◊G◊HM◊

armogonma

3. One of Link's allies is possessed and becomes this terror of Snowpeak Ruins.

BL◊ZZ◊T◊

BLizzeta

4. Link must rely on his Clawshot to rid the Lakebed Temple of this leviathan.

M◊RPH◊◊L

morpheel

5. This monster was a lifeless skeleton buried in the Arbiter's Grounds until the Scimitar of Twilight brought it back to life.

ST◊LL◊RD

stallord

Despite the ever-present danger of the Twilight Realm, the people of Hyrule live interesting lives even if they're *not* heroes of legend. Imagine you lived in Link's world. What profession might you have?

Create a character for yourself. Are you a **HYLIAN**, a **GORON**, or a **ZORA**?
Write about how you would help Link defeat Ganon.

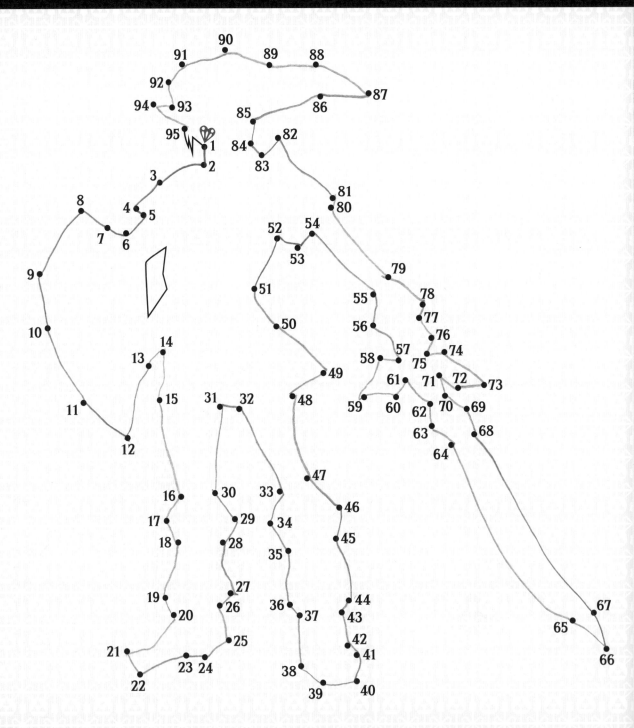

30

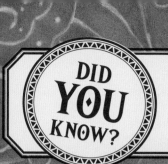

Link is assisted throughout *The Legend of Zelda: Twilight Princess* by Midna. Midna also appears in the Super Smash Bros. series as a mischievous assist trophy, adding chaos to the mix.

People of the GREAT SEA tell tales of a sunken city and lost treasure. On OUTSET ISLAND, boys dress all in green like the HERO OF TIME. When young Link comes of age, he dons his new outfit and sails off on a mighty adventure!

Study the scene on the left for up to three minutes; then cover the page and try to answer these questions.

1. Who is soaring through the sky over Ganon's right shoulder?

_____

2. What symbol is on the top pirate flag in the background?

_____

3. Only one of Ganon's eyes is visible—which one?

_____

4. Is Tetra on Link's right side or left side?

_____

5. Link is guiding the winds with the Wind Waker.
In which hand is he holding it?

_____

6. The Helmaroc King is a massive bird.
How many tail feathers does it have?

_____

7. What color is Tetra's vest?

_____

Link crosses troubled waters on the **KING OF RED LIONS**,
a talking sailboat that often offers sage advice.
Which path will steer Link through the wild waves?

A

B

C

FINISH

34

Near the end of *The Legend of Zelda: The Wind Waker*, Link discovers a secret about the *King of Red Lions* that explains how the boat can speak the ancient Hylian language!

"TINGLE, TINGLE! KOOLOO-LIMPAH!"

TINGLE
KEY

TINGLE TANGLE

TINGLE is an unusual fellow who obsesses over making himself richer.
Along with his siblings, ANKLE, KNUCKLE, and DAVID JR.,
Tingle often offers to sell Link items at marked-up prices!

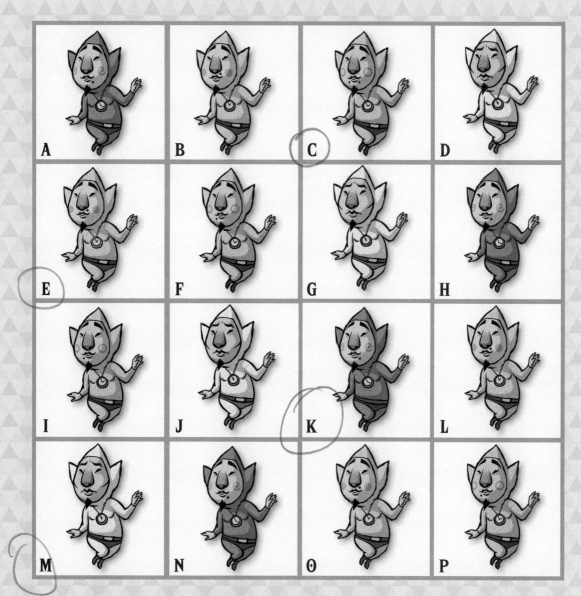

One of each of the Tingle siblings above is an imposter planted by
Ganon to sell Link booby-trapped items! The key on the facing page
shows the correct Tingles. Circle each of the pretenders.

TETRA may act bossy, but she's a caring young pirate captain, and is respected by her older crew. She also has a surprising destiny, as Link discovers during the course of his journey on the Great Sea.

As leader of the pirates, *you* are in charge of the ship! Make a list of essential items needed on board. What will your crew eat? How will they defend themselves? What is needed to repair any damage your ship sustains during battle?

Once you've made your list of must-have supplies, design your own pirate flag. Will your flag strike terror in the hearts of your enemies or make them laugh and signal friendship?

Link's great battles and triumphs are immortalized in stained-glass windows.
Create a stained-glass image of one of your finest moments.
Use bold black lines and striking colors.

DID
YOU
KNOW?

The Wind Waker was the first game
in The Legend of Zelda series to
use a cel-shaded cartooning style!

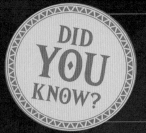

Link transforms into different shapes by wearing masks imbued with magic. These forms help him do things he can't do as a regular Hylian, like breathe underwater. Help Link figure out when to wear each mask by unscrambling these names.

1. This mask helps Link swim swiftly underwater and turns his ocarina into a fishbone guitar.

S Z A A O R K M

Zora
mask

2. While wearing this mask, Link can shoot bubbles and use flowers to fly.

M K K U D E A S

Deku
mask

3. If Link has to walk on lava or roll around at top speed, this is the mask he uses.

N S O O R G M A K

Goroh
mask

4. This is the final and most powerful mask Link obtains. He uses its mighty double blade to defeat the most fearsome bosses.

R E E C F I   S I D E T Y   K A S M

Fierce
Deity's
mask

THE SKULL KID is an imp who long ago befriended the **FOUR GIANTS**, the guardian deities of **TERMINA**. When the four giants decided to split the land equally and guard each section in their slumber, the Skull Kid felt angry and rejected. He later stole the powerful—and evil— **MAJORA'S MASK** and used its magic to draw the moon toward Termina, threatening to destroy the entire world.

Link must play several songs to stop the Skull Kid's wicked plot.

Use the key to decipher the song titles.

H	R	S	E	L	O	M	N	F	G	T	I	A	D

1. SONG of TIME

2. OATH TO ORDER

3. SONG of HEALING

The land of Termina is full of unusual characters.

The petite ZUBORA and the hulking GABORA are blacksmiths in the snowy mountains. They'll help Link upgrade his sword—for a fee. Although it seems Gabora does all the work while Zubora kicks back and relaxes. . . .

The ROSA SISTERS, MARILLA and JUDO, need Link's help practicing their dance moves. The master dancer KAMARO died before he could pass on his skills, and only by donning Kamaro's Mask can Link channel his talent and instruct the Rosa Sisters.

No one knows whose hand this is, only that it reaches out of the toilet of the STOCK POT INN every night at midnight, begging for paper! Link should be a pal and help the guy out. . . .

DID YOU KNOW?

A mysterious hand also pops out of a toilet at the Knight Academy in *Skyward Sword*!

MASKED JUNGLE WARRIOR

ODOLWA haunts Woodfall Temple and wields a sword several times larger than Link. He has captured the DEKU PRINCESS in addition to one of the giants.

MASKED MECHANICAL MONSTER

GOHT storms through Snowhead Temple. He has cursed Snowhead to endure unending winter, which threatens the Gorons who call the mountain home.

GARGANTUAN MASKED FISH

GYORG has polluted the waters of Great Bay Temple, wrecking the surrounding climate and the ecosystem of the Zora people.

GIANT MASKED INSECT

TWINMOLD is responsible for the destruction of IKANA CANYON, turning the region into an empty, haunted realm.

Link changes form based on the mask he wears,
and each form plays a different type of instrument.
Color the Deku form.

Color the Zora form.

Color the Goron form.

Do you play any
instruments?
Which would
you like to learn—
the horns of the Deku,
the drums of the Goron,
or the fishbone guitar
of the Zora?
Why?

Link is only a young boy when he begins having nightmares about a princess fleeing from an evil man clad all in black. To fulfill his heroic destiny, Link must become the Hero of Time, crossing not just Hyrule but time itself to grow into a brave young man and confront Hyrule's dark future.

Draw your vision of your future self.
Maybe you'll remember to look back at it
in a few years to see if you were right.

Princess Zelda wields powerful magic to keep her kingdom safe. To secretly aid Link in his quest, Zelda disguises herself as the stealthy SHEIK. As Sheik, Zelda throws explosive DEKU NUTS to create smoke clouds and cover her quick escapes.

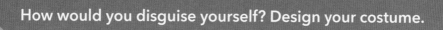

How would you disguise yourself? Design your costume.

EPONA is Link's loyal steed, but she didn't start off friendly—Link had to earn her trust and learn a song on his ocarina to soothe her temper. Feeding her carrots didn't hurt, either. Guide them through the maze.

START

FINISH

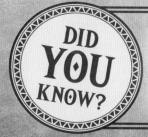

Ocarina of Time may be the highest-rated video game of *all time*. The first game to get a perfect 40/40 from the respected Japanese magazine *Famitsu,* it also holds a Guinness World Record for the Most Critically Acclaimed Game of All Time.

Although Link is not actually one of the KOKIRI people, the GREAT DEKU TREE bestows upon him a personal guardian fairy named NAVI to accompany him on his quest. Navi helps draw Link's attention to items, enemies, and challenges in the world around him.

**Draw your own guardian fairy.
What is your fairy's name?**

Fin peek

Ganon presents a terrifying threat to the kingdom of Hyrule, but he's not the only monstrous force Link must overcome to protect his home. Use the code to uncover the names of the bosses that lie in wait at the end of each temple on his journey.

A	B	C	D	E	F	G	H	I	J	K	L	M	N	O	P	Q	R	S	T	U	V	W	X	Y	Z
Z	Y	X	W	V	U	T	S	R	Q	P	O	N	M	L	K	J	I	H	G	F	E	D	C	B	A

1. **E L O E Z T R Z**
Volvagia

2. **O R A Z O U L H**
Lizalfos

3. **H G Z O U L H**
Stalfos

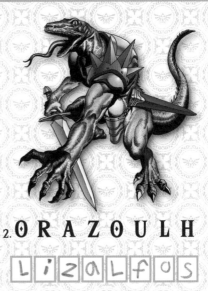

4. **Y Z I R M Z W V**
Barinade

5. W V P F Y Z Y Z

DEKU BABA

6. G D R M I L E Z

twinrova

7. T L S N Z

Gohma

8. W L W L M T L

DODONGO

You began your journey by designing your heroic weapon, but Link must call upon the strength of his shield to survive Ganon's assault—and a hero's goal is to defend, not only to attack. Design a crest for your shield.

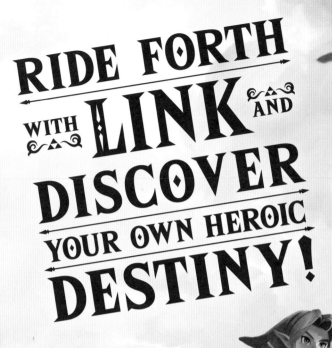

RIDE FORTH
WITH LINK AND
DISCOVER
YOUR OWN HEROIC
DESTINY!

ANSWERS

PAGE 11

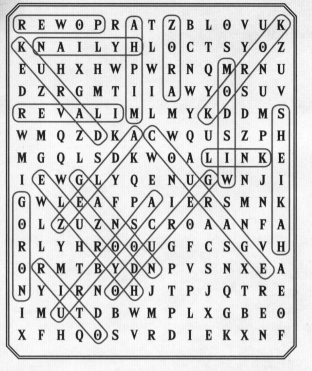

```
R E W O P R A T Z B L O V U K
K N A I L Y H L O C T S Y O Z
E U H X H W P W R N Q M R N U
D Z R G M T I I A W Y O S U V
R E V A L I M L M Y K D D M S
W M Q Z D K A C W Q U S Z P H
M G Q L S D K W O A L I N K E
I E W G L Y Q E N U G W N J I
G W L E A F P A I E R S M N K
O L Z U Z N S C R O A A N F A
R L Y H R O O U G F C S G V H
O R M T B Y D N P V S N X E A
N Y I R N O H J T P J Q T R E
I M U T D B W M P L X G B E O
X F H Q O S V R D I E K X N F
```

PAGE 15

DOWN

1. SKULLTULA
2. STALFOS
3. FI
4. GHIRAHIM
5. CRIMSON
6. ZELDA

ACROSS

1. HYLIA
2. SKYLOFT
3. LOFTWING
4. THE IMPRISONED
5. DEMISE
6. TRIFORCE

PAGE 18

SHEIKAH EYE SYMBOL

PAGE 20

KNIGHT ACADEMY

PAGE 23

1. Four
2. Red
3. Green
4. Front left
5. Left
6. Sword, left
7. Right

PAGE 27

1. ARGOROK
2. ARMOGOHMA
3. BLIZZETA
4. MORPHEEL
5. STALLORD

PAGE 24

```
B O K F O S G O H M A D E A D
X K O L A N Y G R A K E I N K
R E B L I N D A R O K R G H T
E L A L U T L L A W L L U K S
M I Z A L F O S K E E S E S T
M B A B U K E D D N U O H L A
A A L L T U L A S T A L F O S
H S U R E T B B U B D R A Z T
K H K A A S L E D O D O N E O
R A S L D A M R A Y A U G E R
A D T F A E O S S K U G O R C
D O S O O V Q I Z X L L G F H
M W A S T U K E D T U K U L S
R B E M T S D A R K N I U Q A
O D L O A R L U O H G D T L L
```

PAGE 33

1. Valoo
2. Skull and crossbones
3. Left
4. Right
5. Left
6. Three
7. Blue

PAGE 34

C

PAGE 37

C, E, K, M

PAGE 43

1. ZORA MASK
2. DEKU MASK
3. GORON MASK
4. FIERCE DEITY'S MASK

PAGE 45

1. SONG OF TIME
2. OATH TO ORDER
3. SONG OF HEALING

PAGES 60-61

1. VOLVAGIA
2. LIZALFOS
3. STALFOS
4. BARINADE
5. DEKU BABA
6. TWINROVA
7. GOHMA
8. DODONGO

PAGE 56